THIS BOOK
BELONGS TO

_____

_____

by monica sheehan

be happy!

a little book
for a happy you
and a better
world

LITTLE SIMON
New York   London   Toronto   Sydney   New Delhi

LITTLE SIMON

An imprint of Simon & Schuster Children's Publishing Division
1230 Avenue of the Americas, New York, New York 10020
Copyright © 2010 by Monica Sheehan. First jacketed hardcover edition, 2014
All rights reserved, including the right of reproduction in whole or
in part in any form. Little Simon is a registered trademark of Simon & Schuster, Inc.,
and associated colophon is a trademark of Simon & Schuster, Inc.
For information about special discounts for bulk purchases,
please contact Simon & Schuster Special Sales at 1-866-506-1949
or business@simonandschuster.com. The Simon & Schuster Speakers Bureau can bring authors
to your live event. For more information or to book an event contact
the Simon & Schuster Speakers Bureau at 1-866-248-3049 or
visit our website at www.simonspeakers.com.
Also available in a Little Simon board book edition.
Designed by Monica Sheehan
Manufactured in China 0516 SCP
4 6 8 10 9 7 5
ISBN 978-1-4424-9857-0 (HC)
ISBN 978-1-4424-0676-6 (board)
ISBN 978-1-4424-4974-9 (eBook)

for jack

SING  and

DA

NCE

a little!

DRaw

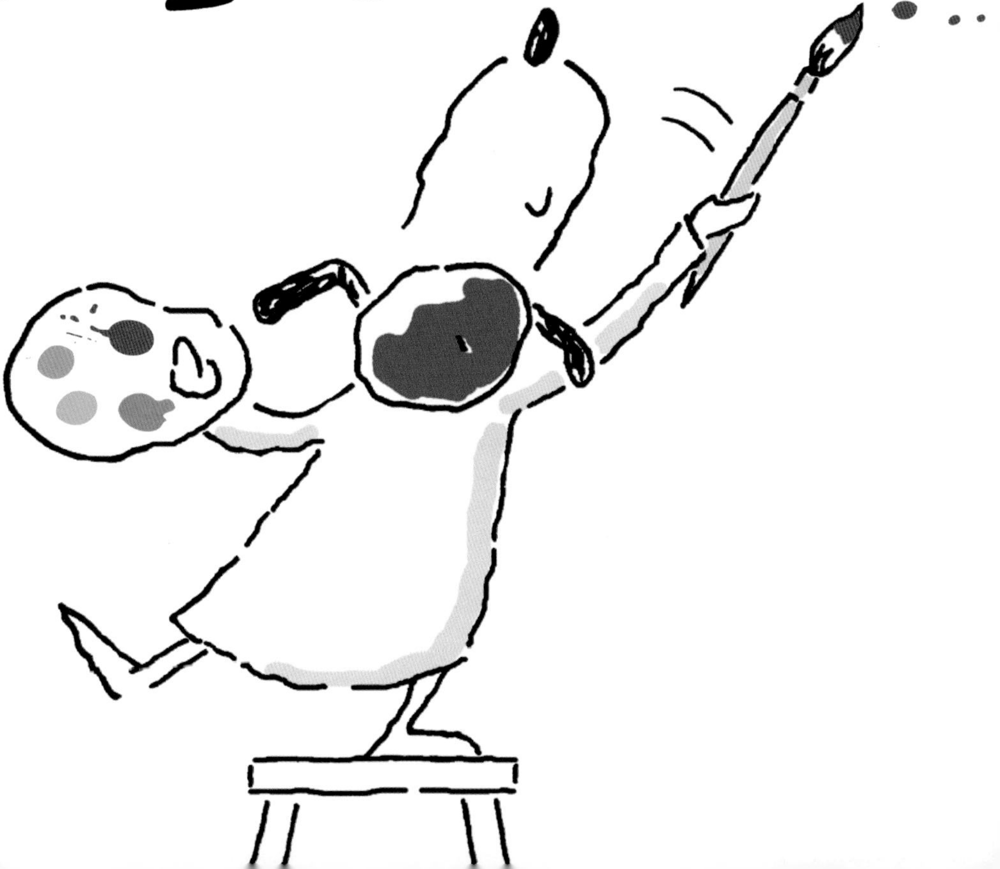

and

PAINT

a little...

Make

Don't compare

...with

YOURSELF

OTHERS.

BE THE BEST

YOU!

helpful!

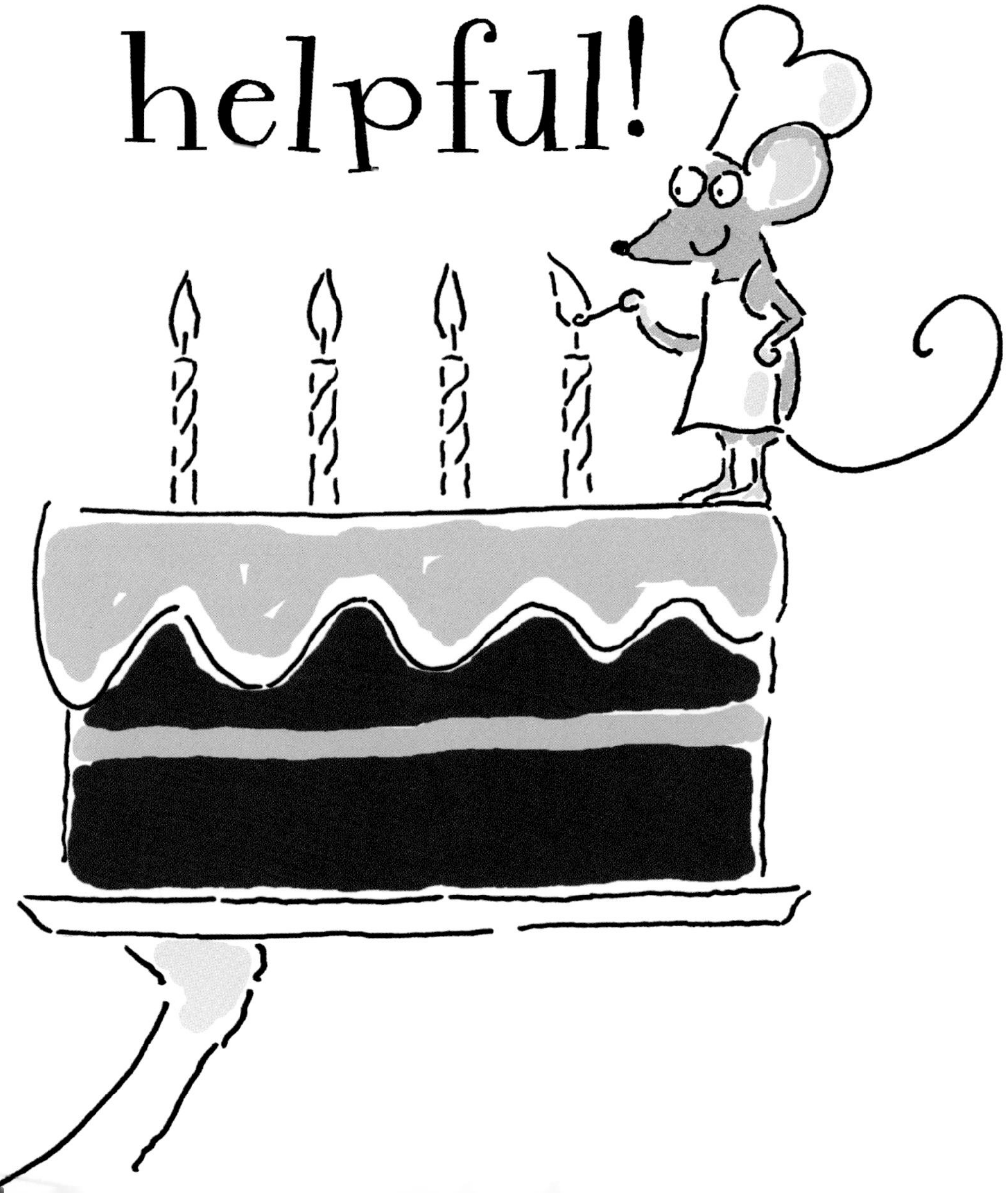

Be Cu

RIO us.

Be Br

STAND

FOR YOURSELF
...AND OTHERS.

Be a

HERO!...

for MOTHER EARTH.

Say...

THANK

TO THE PEOPLE
THAT TEACH YOU...
HELP YOU...
CHEER YOU ON...

YOU

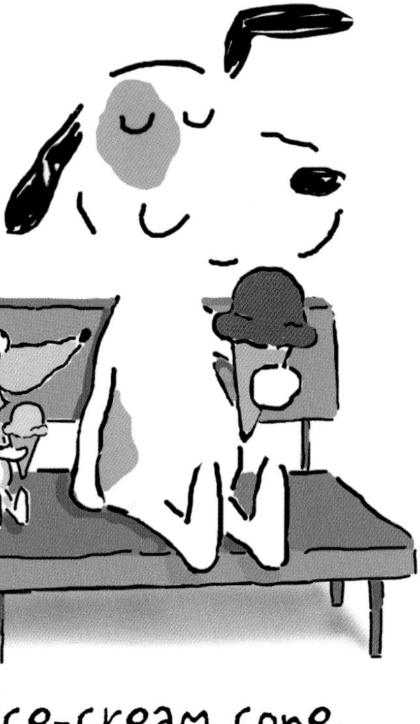

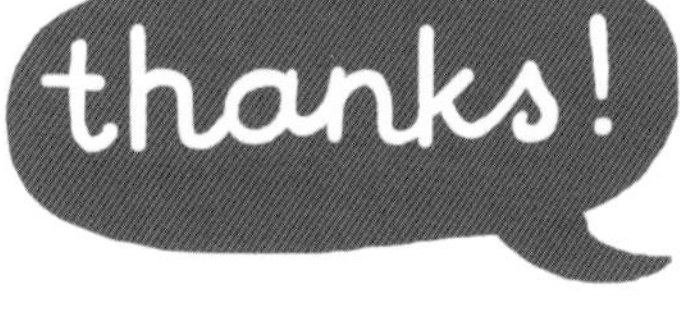

and get you an ice-cream cone.

UNPLUG
YOURSELF

from the TV . . . and
the video games!!

Go Outside!

PLAY!

EXPLORE.

READ

KEEP LEARNING!

books.

F. SPOT
FITZGERALD

AKES.

The only REAL mistake
is not TRYING.

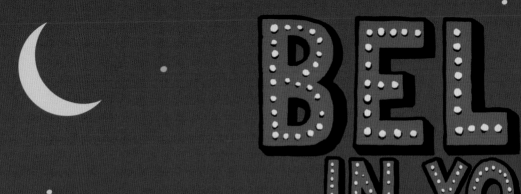

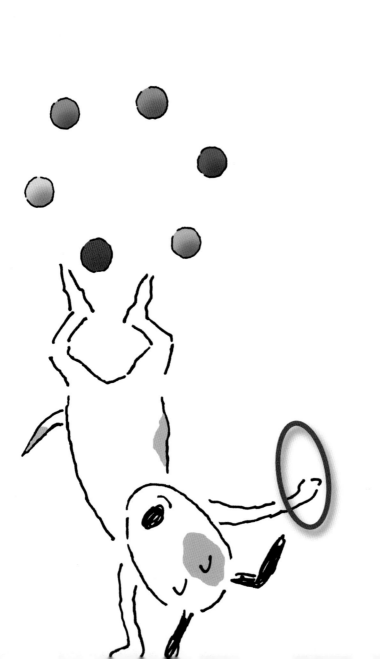

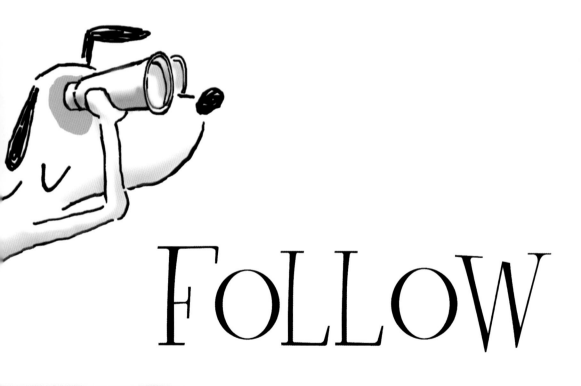

FOLLOW

YOUR

Be
l ki

Be thankful

for ALL the people
and things you LOVE.

You never know what

TOMORROW will bring!

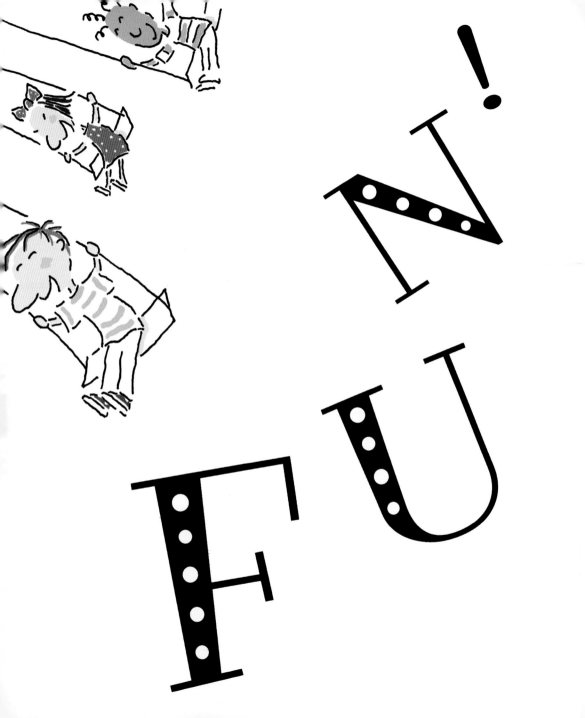

FUN!

Make the world

a better place!

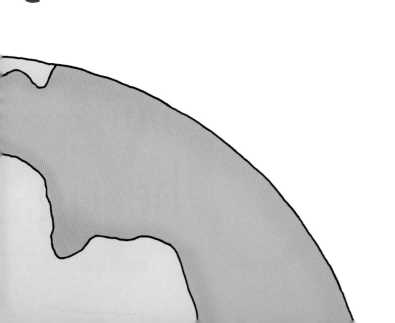

Can you THINK
of some things

? you're happy about right NOW?

things i'm thankful for...

_____

_____

_____

_____

_____

_____

_____

_____

my dreams are...

_____

_____

_____